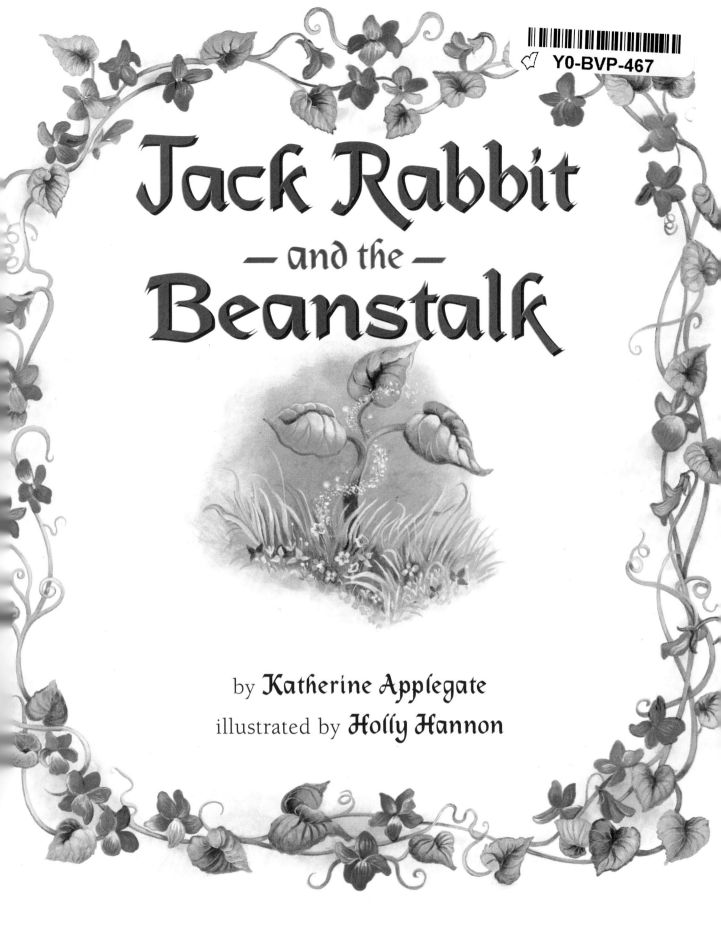

Jack Rabbit
— and the —
Beanstalk

by **Katherine Applegate**

illustrated by **Holly Hannon**

There was nothing Jack Rabbit loved better than a fine, fat carrot. He loved tall-as-his-ears carrots. Stubby-as-his-tail carrots. Round-as-his-tummy carrots. He loved carrot muffins and carrot stew and especially carrot ice cream.

Jack was so busy eating all his carrots that he forgot to plant more. One morning, when he pushed his wheelbarrow out to the garden, his carrot patch was empty.

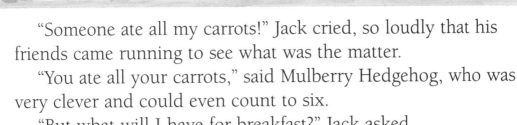

"Someone ate all my carrots!" Jack cried, so loudly that his friends came running to see what was the matter.

"You ate all your carrots," said Mulberry Hedgehog, who was very clever and could even count to six.

"But what will I have for breakfast?" Jack asked.

"Honey always hits the spot," suggested Briar Bear.

"There's nothing like a nice bowl of berries to start the day," added Mulberry.

"Stewed cabbage and brussels sprouts," said Pepper the skunk. "Nothing smells as heavenly!"

Jack groaned. None of that sounded nearly as good as his delicious carrots.

"There's just one thing to do," said Mulberry. "You must sell your wheelbarrow at the market. Then you can buy some more carrots."

Jack knew a good idea when he heard one. He set out at once for the market. He was almost there when he came across an old fox sitting under a tree.

"That's a mighty nice wheelbarrow," said the fox. "I'd like to buy it from you."

"How much will you give me for it?" Jack asked.

"I'll give you something better than money," said the fox. "I'll give you these magic beans!"

Jack had to admit they were fine-looking beans. They shimmered like gold in the bright morning sun.

"Will they grow carrots?" he asked.

"Better than carrots," said the fox. "These beans grow magic."

Jack knew a good offer when he heard one. He made the trade and ran all the way home. He couldn't wait to tell his friends about his magic beans!

"How much did you get for the wheelbarrow?" asked Mulberry.

"I traded it for something better than money," Jack said proudly. He handed Mulberry the magic beans.

"Beans?" Mulberry cried.

"Those aren't just any beans," Jack said. "Those are magic beans."

"Jack," Mulberry said, "there's no such thing as magic beans."

"Are you positively, absolutely sure?" Jack asked.

Mulberry nodded. "Have you ever known me to be wrong?" With that, she tossed the beans right out the window.

That night there was no carrot cake for Jack. He crawled into bed, feeling miserable and hungry.

The next morning, Jack looked out the window and noticed something very strange. Very strange, very green, and very, very big . . . .

It was an
enormous
beanstalk!

"So they really were magic beans," Jack said.

Naturally, he had to see where the beanstalk went. Jack had climbed halfway to the clouds when he heard familiar voices calling out from far below. He looked down and saw Mulberry, Briar, and Pepper waving at him.

"Jack!" Mulberry cried. "Come back!"

But Jack knew an adventure when he saw one. He just waved back and continued to climb. At last he came to the top of the beanstalk. A blanket of clouds spread as far as the eye could see. Towering above Jack was a huge stone castle.

Jack sneaked into the castle through a crack in the kitchen door. Suddenly a horrible thunderous sound filled the air. Jack hid in a cupboard just as a huge, ugly giant stomped into the room.

"Fee fi fo funny!" he cried. "I smell the blood of a curious bunny!"

"I love a good bunny stew," the giant thundered, sniffing the air hungrily as he searched high and low for Jack.

At last he gave up. He opened a cage that held a fat white goose.

"Lay!" the giant commanded, setting her on the table.

A minute later, an egg lay on the table. But it was not just any egg. This egg was made of pure gold!

How I'd love to have a goose that lays golden eggs! Jack thought. Then I could buy all the carrots I'll ever need.

Jack waited patiently until the giant had fallen asleep at the kitchen table. Each snore shook the whole castle.

Carefully Jack slipped out of the cupboard and grabbed the goose.

Honk! she said, startled.

The giant awoke with a start. "Fee fi fo foose!" he cried. "Someone has stolen my favorite goose!"

Out of the castle and across the clouds Jack dashed with the goose under his arm. Behind him the giant loomed. With each step the clouds trembled.

The beanstalk was just ahead. Suddenly Mulberry popped up through the clouds. Briar was right behind her.

Mulberry's eyes went wide. "J-J-J-Jack," she cried. "There's a g-g-g-g-g-giant after you!"

"Turn around!" Jack cried. "Go back!"

But it was too late. The giant reached down and scooped up Jack, Mulberry, and Briar in his huge hand.

"Mmm," he said in a booming voice. "Snack time!"

"Uh-oh," said Jack. He knew a hungry giant when he saw one.

"At least Pepper got away," Mulberry whispered as the giant smacked his lips.

Just then a tiny voice called from below, "Hey, where is everybody?"

The giant gave a deafening laugh. He bent down to peer at Pepper.

"There's nothing I like more than a nice, juicy—" Suddenly the giant stopped. He gulped. He took a step back. "SK-SK-SK-SK-SKUNK!" he screeched.

He threw up his hands in terror and lumbered away as fast as he could. Jack, Mulberry, and Briar flew through the air, straight toward the beanstalk. They tumbled head over heels through the clouds. One by one, they grabbed onto the leaves of the beanstalk. Jack even managed to hold onto the magic goose.

A moment later a head poked through the clouds. "Hi, everybody," Pepper said. "Sorry I was late. I'm not a very good climber."

"Fee fi fo funks," said Jack with a smile. "It's a good thing that giant is not fond of skunks!"

The goose laid lots of golden eggs, and soon Jack had all the carrots he could ever want. He invited his friends to a big party, complete with carrot cakes and carrot pies and carrot juice and even just plain carrots.

"I still don't understand why you followed me," Jack said. He looked out the window at the beanstalk, which had already started to blend in with the scenery.

Mulberry spoke for all of them. "Simple. You're our friend. And friends stick by each other, no matter what."

Jack gave everybody another helping of carrot ice cream. He knew good friends when he saw them.